Harry the Hopper

Harry loves to hop, and believes he is a 'hopper' – but not everyone agrees …

This picture book targets the /h/ sound and is part of *Speech Bubbles 2*, a series of picture books that target specific speech sounds within the story.

The series can be used for children receiving speech therapy, for children who have a speech sound delay/disorder, or simply as an activity for children's speech sound development and/or phonological awareness. They are ideal for use by parents, teachers or caregivers.

Bright pictures and a fun story create an engaging activity perfect for sound awareness.

Picture books are sold individually, or in a pack. There are currently two packs available – *Speech Bubbles 1* and *Speech Bubbles 2.* Please see further titles in the series for stories targeting other speech sounds.

Melissa Palmer is a Speech Language Therapist. She worked for the Ministry of Education, Special Education in New Zealand from 2008 to 2013, with children aged primarily between 2 and 8 years of age. She also completed a diploma in children's writing in 2009, studying under author Janice Marriott, through the New Zealand Business Institute. Melissa has a passion for articulation and phonology, as well as writing and art, and has combined these two loves to create *Speech Bubbles*.

What's in the pack?

User Guide

Vinnie the Dove

Rick's Carrot

Harry the Hopper

Have You Ever Met a Yeti?

Zack the Buzzy Bee

Asher the Thresher Shark

Catch That Chicken!

Will the Wolf

Magic Licking Lollipops

Jasper the Badger

Platypus and Fly

The Dragon Drawing War

Harry the Hopper

Targeting the /h/ Sound

Melissa Palmer

Routledge
Taylor & Francis Group

LONDON AND NEW YORK

First published 2021
by Routledge
2 Park Square, Milton Park, Abingdon, Oxon OX14 4RN

and by Routledge
52 Vanderbilt Avenue, New York, NY 10017

Routledge is an imprint of the Taylor & Francis Group, an informa business

British Library Cataloguing-in-Publication Data
A catalogue record for this book is available from the British Library

Library of Congress Cataloging-in-Publication Data
A catalog record has been requested for this book

ISBN: 978-1-138-59784-6 (set)
ISBN: 978-0-367-64855-8 (pbk)
ISBN: 978-1-003-12659-1 (ebk)

Typeset in Calibri
by Newgen Publishing UK

Harry the Hopper

Harry the Hopper loved to hop.

He hopped high and low – he hopped fast and slow!

Harry was happy. He thought he was the best hopper in the world!

Hop hop hop hop!

One day **H**arry felt lonely. So away **h**e **h**opped to find a new friend, who **h**opefully **h**opped too. What **h**opping adventures they could **h**ave together!

Harry met a grasshopper.

"**H**ello! My name is **H**arry, and I am a **h**opper! **Wh**o are you?" said **H**arry.

"My name is **H**annah and I am a grasshopper. You are not a **h**opper! You are a frog!" said **H**annah the grasshopper.

"No! I am a **h**opper! I **h**op **h**igh, I **h**op low, I **h**op fast and I can **h**op slow!"

Harry **h**opped **h**igh into the air to show **H**annah.

"There is no such thing as a **h**opper. I am a GRASSHOPPER. YOU are a FROG."

Hannah **h**opped away in a **h**uff. She didn't look where she was **h**opping!

SPLASH! **H**annah fell into a pond!

"**H**elp me! **H**elp me!" **H**annah couldn't swim!

"**H-h-h-h-h-** help!"

Harry hopped into the water to help Hannah.

He pulled her to safety.

"Thank you, **H**arry. You are not a grasshopper like me, but you can swim! I will call you a **h**opper from now on if you want me to," said **H**annah.

"Let's be friends then. Come to my **h**ouse for tea!" said **H**arry the **H**opper.

They **h**eld **h**ands and **h**opped all the way to **H**arry's **h**ouse for tea.

Harry and **H**annah were both very **h**appy.